For Rocco!
I love you,
Aunt Tricia

TOP SECRET

TOP SECRET

powered by:

CARDBOARD

draw · cut out · stick

$x\sqrt{\dfrac{3 \times 2}{18}}$

$\begin{array}{r} 3.950 \\ \times 8.19 \\ \hline \end{array}$

2+2+2+2=8

$y\sqrt{8+10087219}$

1. 2. 3. 4. 7.

a b c

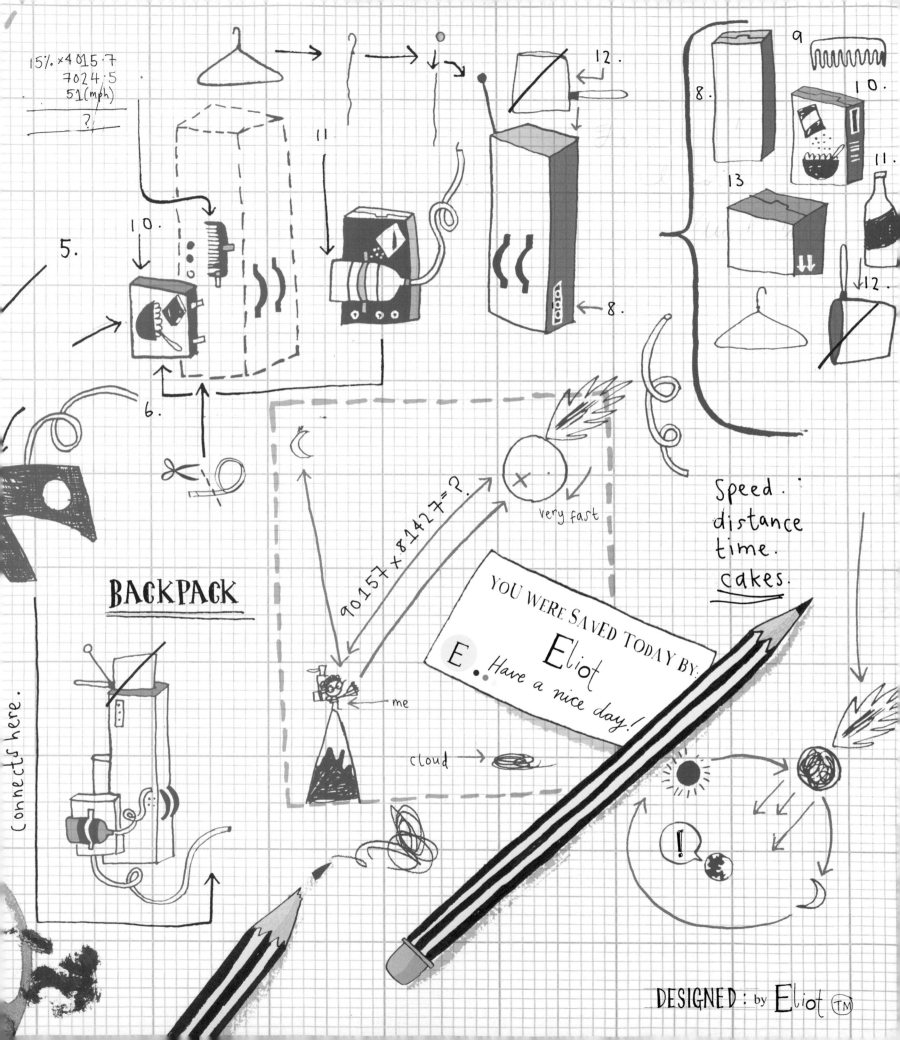

For my three forever superheroes: Richard, Joe, and Freddy –A.C.

For my heroes: Georgia, Thomas, and Jemma –A.T.S

tiger tales
an imprint of ME Media, LLC
202 Old Ridgefield Road, Wilton, CT 06897
Published in the United States 2009
Originally published in Great Britain 2008
by Scholastic Children's Books,
a division of Scholastic Books Ltd.
Text copyright ©2008 Anne Cottringer
Illustrations copyright ©2008 Alex T. Smith
CIP data is available
Printed in Singapore
Hardcover ISBN-13: 978-1-58925-083-3
Hardcover ISBN-10: 1-58925-083-4
Paperback ISBN-13: 978-1-58925-416-9
Paperback ISBN-10: 1-58925-416-3

by Anne Cottringer

Illustrated by Alex T. Smith

ELIOT JONES, MIDNIGHT SUPERHERO

tiger tales

By day, Eliot is quiet.
He reads his books.
He feeds his goldfish.
He watches Mr. Smith
wash his car.

TIBET

TOY BOX

"Eliot is such a quiet little thing," say **all** the grown-ups.

Tick! Tock! Tick! Tock! Tick! Tock!

BONG!

But when the clock strikes *midnight*...

Eliot is a Superhero!

He hangs out of helicopters.

He skis down glaciers.

He returns teddy bears to babies.

Eliot

Sometimes the mayor needs Eliot's help. "The lions have escaped from the zoo!" he cries. "They're rampaging through the streets!"

Luckily, Eliot is an expert lion tamer.

He leaps from his bedroom window, races through the screaming crowds...

and comes face to face with the lions.
He stares into the eyes of the
ROARING beasts.

One by one,
Eliot stops them
in their tracks.

He leads the
lions back
to the zoo…

as the crowds cheer.

ZOO

Sometimes the
Coast Guard calls
on his services.

"Help!" they shout.
"A ship is about to CRASH
onto the rocks!"

Luckily, Eliot is a
champion swimmer.

THE RUBBER DUCKY

He dives into the towering waves,
grabs the anchor, and tows the ship to safety,
as the sailors shout "Hooray!"

Sometimes the queen requires his assistance.

"A criminal mastermind has **stolen** the royal jewels!" announces the royal butler.

Luckily, Eliot is an excellent sleuth.

He sneaks into the criminal mastermind's secret hideout.

Tiptoe!

He follows the clues, cracks the code, opens the safe...

and returns the jewels to the grateful queen.

Tonight, Eliot receives an urgent message from the world's most important scientists.

"A gigantic METEOR is heading this way! It's going to SMASH into the Earth!"

This is Eliot's most dangerous mission ever

Luckily, Eliot has built a Meteor-Busting Rocket Launcher for just such occasions.

Unluckily, it's hidden in a deep cave in the Himalayan Mountains of **TIBET**.

The only way to get there before the meteor strikes is by supersonic jet.

Luckily, Eliot is a skilled jet pilot.

Eliot sets off.
Over the Atlantic.
Down to the Arabian Sea.
Across to the Himalayas.

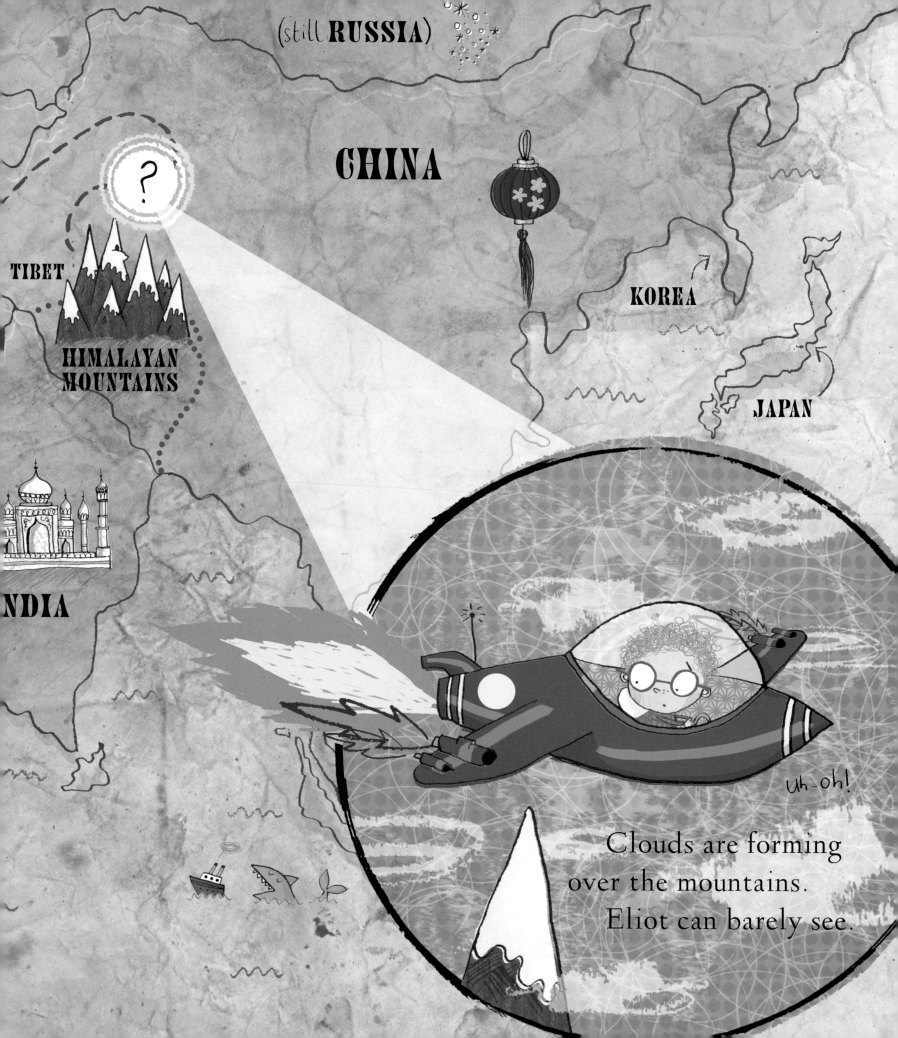

(still RUSSIA)

CHINA

TIBET

KOREA

HIMALAYAN
MOUNTAINS

JAPAN

?

INDIA

Uh-oh!

Clouds are forming
over the mountains.
Eliot can barely see.

Suddenly, a snow-capped peak flashes past his window. Another looms up straight ahead.

Eliot dips his left wing and swerves just in time.

!

To reach the cave, he must now land on the shortest, most dangerous runway in the world.

He grips the controls.
The wheels bump
the ground.

Screeech!

Eliot skids to a halt.

The sky is blazing with the light of the meteor.

Closer
and
closer
it comes.

Eliot can see the entrance to the cave, far above him. Luckily, Eliot is a highly experienced mountaineer. He scrambles up the cliff face and into the cave.

Eliot swings the barrel of the Meteor-Busting Rocket Launcher toward the sky.

He aims.
He holds his breath.
He waits until just the right moment.

He fires!

KAPOW!

Eliot saves the world from destruction!

Hooray!

That was close!

The queen gives Eliot an award for his courage and ingenuity.

The Earth trembles with deafening applause.

But being a Midnight Superhero is very tiring.

It doesn't leave Eliot with much energy.

So by day...

Eliot is quiet.

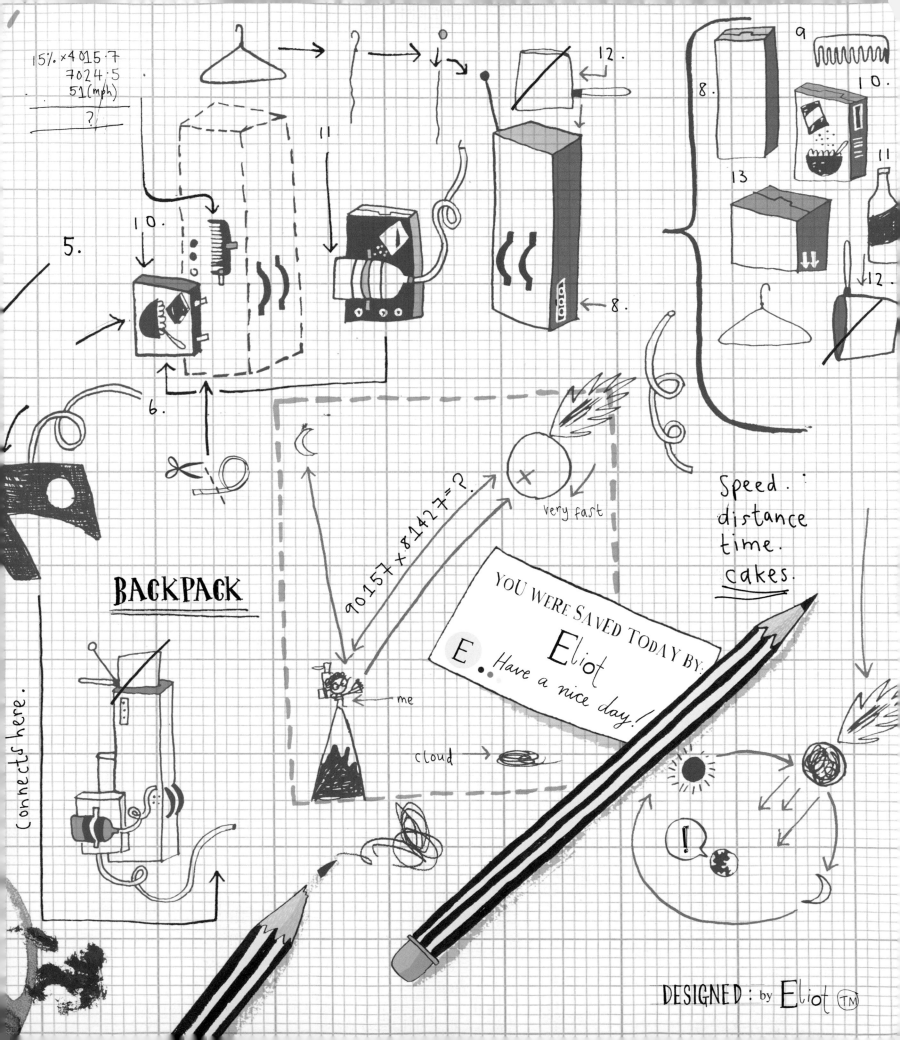